A Test of Fayth

Heart of a Wounded Hero

Melverna McFarlane

McFarlane Publishing, LLC

Author's Note

Please be aware that this story involves sensitive topics listed below. If you consider such warnings to be spoilers, please skip ahead and enjoy Keoni and Fayth's journey.

- Childhood neglect
- OCD
- Dealing with death of a loved one

Keep up with Melverna McFarlane

Join Melverna McFarlane's newsletter to get updates, bonus scenes, and more. Click here or go to http://melvernamcfarlane.com/a-test-of-fayth-pleasure-seeker/ to join my newsletter and get a free novella.

As always, I'd like to thank my family Craig, Woodrow, Patrece and Rozzeann for pushing me to believe in my dream even when I doubted myself; my friends Ginelle, Cindy, and Nala who provided great critiques; and to everyone reading this who enjoys the journey into my imagination.

Proud supporter of Semper Fi & America's Fund. Semper Fi & America's Fund cares for our nation's critically wounded ill, and injured service members and military families. Supporting all branches of the U.S. Armed Forces, they provide one-on-one case management, connection, and lifetime support. Today. Tomorrow. Together.

The Heart of the Wounded Hero series was created to pay tribute to and raise awareness of our wounded heroes. Each of the over eighty authors involved have contributed time, money, and stories to the cause. These love stories are inspiring and uplifting, showing the sacrifice of our veterans but also giving them the happily ever after they deserve.

By increasing awareness through our books, we believe we can in a small part help the wounded heroes that have sacrificed so much. To see all the books in the series and to support Semper Fi & America's Fund, please go to: https://heartofawoundedhero.com/

Chapter One

Dear John,

   I feel like I always have to preface my letters to you by saying this isn't one of those Dear John letters. Don't mind my sense of humor, it will grow on you. I hope you are well and keeping as safe as you can considering you put your life on the line to protect people like me every day.

   You probably have people worrying about you a lot. That and thanking you for your service. Well, just add me to the list. Learning about your mom supporting you really hit home for me because I can't always rely on my family to have my back. I'm happy you have that kind of support and you deserve it.

   By the way, you can add a kindergarten full of kids as new fans. I hope you don't mind, but I mentioned I had a pen pal in the marines to my kids and they went over the moon about you. Like super-charged sugar-high level.

   Have you ever seen a five-year-old when the sweets kick in? It's not for the faint of heart.

   I can't complain, though. You've surpassed super-hero

level awesomeness for them. For me too. Not even my not-so-little Maine Coon, Snugglepuss, gets the fandom treatment like you do when they ask me for updates about you. And don't say it's because I fangirl for you. I do, but you don't have to repeat it.

Next time, I'll tell you about some stories they make up, starring...you guessed it. You. I hope they'll entertain you as much as they have me. In the meantime, I've enclosed some of their drawings for you.

Sincerely
Fayth Love

Well wishes and condolences

Lei-clad mourners in bright aloha wear mill through the house and backyard. They share funny stories full of affection and intimate knowledge. While their sorrow-filled joy surrounds me, it becomes too much all of a sudden. I seek a few seconds to pull myself together.

I only need two.

Liar.

Two deep breaths become three, four. With each breath, the sweet-scented maile lei around my neck helps to thin the fog clouding my mind. The murkiness I've been swimming in since I heard of my mother's illness probably won't disappear for a long time, if ever. Right now, these precious seconds will give me the wherewithal to do my duty to my mother, Makana Kekoa, who I laid to rest this morning.

I wasn't ready for her to go. For the past seven years, I'd barely come home, and now I have to face the embodiment of my shame every day.

The haunting voice of my mother's kumu draws me out

to the bustling backyard. People seat themselves on the lawn to listen to the traditional Hawaiian words in the oli.

My heart thuds a bittersweet tune. Like many of my responsibilities, I have allowed distance to separate me from many parts of my culture. As the hālau teacher chants a send-off for my mother, I soak in the moment. Hope springs inside me that the words will help to heal me of this festering wound I've been living with for too long.

As everything winds down, I realize that I've let my mom down again. I walk through the house searching for Vivian, but there is no sign of her.

I stop my mother's long-time neighbor on his way out. "Thank you so much for coming. My mother would be glad to know how well the community remembers her."

"Sure thing, Keoni. She was vital to the neighborhood and so proud of you. She always bragged about her son, the best marine that ever was. Now that you're retired, I hope to see you more often."

"Of course. By the way, have you seen Vivian?"

"Vivi—oh, I forgot. Makana always called her Apikalia. I'm sure I saw your daughter following Faith next door. Your mother hānaied the young woman when she moved into the neighborhood two years ago. Makana had a big heart for everyone, and Faith turned around and adopted your mother, too." He pats me on the shoulder as he leaves.

I can't argue with him. Learning my mother took a stranger in as a daughter is not surprising. She had a soft heart for everybody. My mother was the first to forgive my wife once she couldn't hide her treachery any longer. I should be over what my wife did to me. It's been over six years. Yet rage continues to turn my vision red every time I think about that woman.

In the few seconds I take to clear my head so I can

retrieve Vivian, another funeral goer that I can't place pats my arm, stopping me from leaving.

"Keoni, if you need anything, and I mean anything, you give me call. I no like hear dat you struggling when I stay around the corner."

"Thank you. Right now, I'm looking for Vivian. Someone said she may be at the neighbor's house."

Instead of talking story with me, he nods and lets me pass. On the walk, I try to recall what this woman looks like. I should know since Vivian spends a lot of time with her. The neighbor seems like a nice enough woman. While handling the doctors' visits and keeping my mother comfortable, I haven't had to worry about food. Faith not only organized the neighborhood with routine house cleaning and food drop-offs, she makes the best pasteles on the island.

Despite her generosity to my family, I can't help the resentment springing up inside me. There is still so much to do regarding my mother's estate and finding a new job now that I can no longer serve.

Each item on my list of shit I never wanted to deal with adds fuel to the fire and more weight beneath each step as I stomp past the mango tree filled with ripening fruit. At her front door, I bang, realizing too late that I need to temper my emotions.

I'm used to holding things in and presenting an unbothered front. It comes...came with my job and has helped me avoid situations and questions that could undermine my hard-earned control.

The door swings inward to a vision of gleaming dark brown skin and glossy black curls pulled into a thick pony-tail that takes my breath away. Immediately, I recognize the unique lehua pattern on the dress covering her generous curves because I've seen the back of it so much today. But the dress only helps me place her.

Her face stamps itself in my long-term and short-term memory with one glance. There's no way I'll ever forget her full, rounded cheeks or her pretty nose. Not even the shiny dark eyes narrowing in speculation as I stand speechless.

I know I'm staring and I need to look away or say something, anything to not seem like a creep, but the power to do so has deserted me.

Although she has been on the periphery of my existence over the past three weeks, we've never exchanged words and I've never seen Faith until now. I only know she's stopped by the house from the notes signed with an F that she leaves behind. At first, her mysterious appearance felt intrusive, but after discovering she was my mother's hānai daughter, I had no room to argue.

I shake my head, trying to put a coherent thought together. With everything going on around me, I have no time to pursue anyone. Not when I'm still smarting from the desertion of the woman who almost made me believe in love again.

First my wife and then—

"Keoni?" Her throaty voice has a New York accent, though I can't place which borough, and reminds me of the seconds passing without me saying a word. She licks lips that are in no need of moisture. Could she be attracted to me too? I shake the thought from my mind. I'm not here for her.

"Yes...I'm looking for Vivian. Is she here?"

"Vivian...Apikalia." The question in her eyes clears and with it the beginning haze of desire I have no business wanting to see. She pinches her lips letting me know I've done something wrong, though for the life of me I can't imagine what. "Yes, she's in the backyard keeping my cat company. I'll take you to her."

I remove my slippers as I enter her house, a new irritation growing inside me. I can't put my finger on why, but I sense she isn't my biggest fan. I shrug off the sensation.

Evidence of partially unpacked moving boxes is in every room we pass, reminding me of my previous conversation with my uncle. "My neighbor said you moved here two years ago. How are you liking the island life?"

"A lot, really. It took some getting used to as I moved from the Bronx. As you can see, I haven't found a place for all my stuff yet, but I have a system right now where I know what's in each box."

I nearly stumble when I hear where she's from, but recover quickly.

What are the odds? There's no way.

The Fayth I've known through letters spells her name with a Y. All this time I assumed the F my neighbor signed meant hers had the more common spelling.

I shake my head free of suspicions. The world may be small, but not enough for a coincidental meeting like this. The letters from the Fayth I knew had gotten me through the hardest heartache I've ever experienced. When I thought I was ready to try again with her despite the distance, she ghosted me. And she didn't have the nerve to send me a real Dear John letter first.

We come to the French doors that open to her lānai and I can see Vivian petting and talking to a cat that probably weighs close to twenty pounds. This Faith pauses with her hand on the door handle.

"Look, I know this is probably the worst time to say this, but you aren't the only one who lost someone."

"You're right. It's none of your business."

Faith turns glittering eyes on me. "You're wrong. Apikalia is my business, has been since the moment she asked me if I had to move so far away because my daddy doesn't love me either."

I rear back from the metaphorical slap to my face.

Her eyes widen with guilt and she places her hand on my arm before snatching it away. *Did a bolt travel through her as it did with me?* My skin pulses. I yearn for another caress, no matter how brief.

She clears her throat. "I'm sorry, I know better than to let my emotions fly so freely. If you can't tell, I'm very protective of her, and now that she's lost the only constant presence in her life, I'm particularly sensitive to her needs."

The words to cut her remain lodged in my throat because all my concentration is on the warmth emanating from the brief touch on my arm. As innocent as the physical connection was, it distracts me beyond reason. I like it and want her hand back on my arm where it belongs, although the tongue lashing she is holding back from issuing should rile me.

"It's my job to look after her needs, not yours."

"True, but you've been absent for most of Apikalia's life and she needs you to try harder."

"Her name is Vivian, and you have no idea what I do for her."

"That's fair. And I don't need to know, but Apikalia does. From what she tells me, she doesn't know if she can rely on you."

"Listen, lady, butt out." I storm by her into the yard while she dogs my heels. "I came for Vivian, not a lecture."

Vivian peers up at the sound of my voice, and I can't deny the uncertainty in her eyes or how tightly she grips the large cat to her chest. Shame washes over me at the second reminder today that I am failing my mother.

"Apikalia, amorcita, you're squeezing Snugglepuss really tight."

My neighbor's voice runs down my back like warm molasses until I register the name and I freeze. One name is a coincidence. This cat isn't.

"I'm sorry, Auntie." Vivian leaks contrition and sets the feline down.

"What kind of cat is that?" The words barely leave the constriction of my throat.

Faith, who I'm suspecting is actually Fayth, eyes me warily. "Snugglepuss is my not-so-little Maine Coon." She kneels and the cat goes to her.

"By any chance, is there a Y in your name?" My heartbeat nearly drowns out my words.

Her forehead furrows, but she responds with a hesitant, "...Yes. Most people don't know that unless I tell them."

Shit! This isn't happening.

"Lucky guess," I say as I pick Vivian up and book it to Fayth's front door.

"Listen, I can stop by and help with the clean-up once everyone leaves," her voice follows me outside.

"No need." My throat almost closes at the end of my response. Without stopping to look back, I shut Fayth down. Right now I don't care about being polite, not that I've paid too much attention to niceties during our interaction.

With the past three weeks dealing with my mother's declining health, I have zero capacity to deal with the woman who ghosted me. I'm a coward. Rehashing the empty days and lonely nights where living without Fayth's letters almost broke me worse than my wife's betrayal.

Fayth Love is a danger I need to avoid if I'm going to survive living next door to her.

Not difficult at all.

I ignore the scoff that escapes my lips. Of course, I can resist her and everything she represents. I'm a marine.

Chapter Two

Dear Fayth,

I'm sorry it's taken so long to respond. I just returned from deployment and found your letters. ~~I nearly ripped someone's hand off for touching~~ I've already read them ten times, I was so happy to receive your words and the tidbits from the kids at your school. It made returning after being away for over a year more worthwhile.

Please, never stop writing. Reading about your day helps keep me grounded when I'm among my rowdy brothers-in-arms ~~who play too much when it comes to your letters~~. It just does my heart good overall.

On a hard day, like today, just

seeing your handwriting lifts my spirits. I've reread every letter you've ever sent me to the point that I had to laminate the older ones to preserve them.

I don't mean to gloss over the hard day comment. Like most things, words come so easily when I write to you and for some reason, I prefer to give you the most unsanitized versions of my letters. It's like I need you to see my mistakes because I know you'll accept my flaws without judgment, although we've only been writing to each other for two years.

I digress. Today was particularly hard because it's the anniversary of a traumatic event when someone I used to be close to broke my trust. They're the reason I haven't been home to visit my mother. You'll probably lecture me in your next letter not to let my trust issues come between me and my family, but believe me when I say staying away is the best thing I can do for my mom. She does so much for me. I refuse to enter her home knowing I can't be what she needs me to be. For now, I need to show her my support through other means and distance.

But that's enough about me. I want
to hear more about you and the kids
at your school.

Yours truly,

John Kekoa

Pulling at heartstrings

One day is all I can take before I break down and walk over to Apikalia's house. And it's not because my fingertips continue to tingle from my brief encounter with Keoni.

The six-year-old had never met her mother and, from what Makana told me during the two years I've lived next door, Keoni only visited his daughter long enough to relocate her to Oahu to live with Makana, then bounce. I will never understand the sympathetic way Makana spoke about her son.

That's why I worry for the little girl. As a social worker, I've seen the long-term impact emotional neglect has on kids. Hell, I've been on the receiving end of it. I can't let Apikalia have another childhood like mine.

Is her childhood really like yours, though?

The thought stops me mere steps from the door. Despite Keoni's distant behavior last night, I could chalk his absentmindedness up to his genuine grief for losing his mother.

I'd overheard his fervent prayers when I stopped by to

drop off food for the house. His tortured whispers and failing hope hit me in my too-sensitive heart.

Damn it!

Just remembering the weeks leading up to Makana's passing has my eyes misting over. We connected because she reminded me of my grandmother, the only family who showed up for me when my father couldn't be bothered. With her passing, nothing kept me tied to the Bronx. The similarities I share with Apikalia are a bit unnerving.

Shake it off. You are here to check up on Apikalia, not the overbearing man who breaks down in private when the curtains are down and the place is empty.

I continue down the path but the door swings open and Apikalia launches herself at me. From instinct, my arms wrap around her and I cuddle her shivering body. Alarmed, I listen out to what compelled her to run outside.

When nothing registers, I realize I was expecting the worst of Apikalia's father. Shame at labeling him again without proof engulfs me.

"I did the thing and he won't wake up," Apikalia wails.

I push her away to look her in the eyes. "Amorcita, what thing did you do?"

"I tapped his face three times...was it three times? I can't remember. I have to go back and start over. This time, I'll make sure I do it three times." Apikalia twists out of my arms and runs inside the house.

A sickening feeling grows in my stomach as I follow the little girl inside. I must not jump to conclusions. Any child would exhibit signs of anxiety after losing the person they saw every day. I try to shake off the troubling thoughts circling my head, but they are persistent buggers.

In the living room, Keoni sprawls across the couch asleep. He must be exhausted from the constant worrying.

With his eyes closed, he can't fluster me with his soulful gaze that has seen too many things.

Así es. Idiota!

Fine! The man is a walking fluster machine. His height alone should intimidate me, but despite what I consider my very justified anger towards Apikalia's dad, I feel safe around him. The longer I stare at the comatose man, the more my body reacts, just like it did yesterday.

Maybe safe isn't the right word for what happens to me when I'm around him. His warm, golden complexion and soft curly hair beg me to explore his body with—

"Daddy, please wake up."

Shit!

Apikalia's cry splashes a bucket of shame over me. "Why isn't the tapping working?" Tears glisten on the little girl's lashes, but she bravely holds them back.

I'm here for *her*, not him.

Her tapping is not gentle and I begin to suspect something horrible when his lashes flutter. If not for my acute stare, I would have missed the subtle movement. Instead of stopping Apikalia's actions, I kneel beside her and whisper into Keoni's ear, "Your mother used to tell me what a good man you were, but the man she told me about would not keep distressing his daughter this way."

I take Apikalia's shoulders in my hands. The bones in her tiny body shudder and my heart aches with each shiver running through her. "Amorcita, I need you to breathe with me, OK?"

She nods but continues to poke at Keoni's face in sets of three. I'm not a psychiatrist and diagnosing isn't my job, but I fear Apikalia is exhibiting early signs of an obsessive-compulsive disorder, which is rare in children her age.

Apikalia begins another round of poking when Keoni

gives up the pretense and opens his eyes. What should have been enough to stop her isn't, because she completes the set of three before raising thankful eyes to him.

"Why did it take so long to work?" She turns to me with a determined glint in her eyes. "Three times isn't enough. Four times will do it."

"Four times will do what?" Keoni asks while rising from the couch.

A molten lava flow of rage surges inside me, incinerating my burgeoning attraction to cinders. "Amorcita, can you give me and your dad a few minutes to talk?"

Her gaze bounces between us.

"Why don't you play with Snugglepuss until we're done?" I ask.

She agrees with a concerned frown crinkling her brow and she goes in search of the cat. Apikalia's current circumstances hit far too close to home for me.

As the only child of a single father who was stuck with me when my mother couldn't handle motherhood any longer, I'm afraid this man's lack of empathy for Apikalia's distress will make her feel as unwanted as I've felt most of my life. My grandmother was my buffer, providing joy in an otherwise joyless existence. Apikalia no longer has her buffer, so I will do lo que es necesario for her.

"I thought I could give you the benefit of the doubt, but you pretended to be asleep while your daughter was having a mini breakdown."

A flash of pain runs across his face but he glances away, hiding the glimpse of compassion. Too late. I saw it and I won't let him suppress it.

"Why did you pretend to be asleep?"

He swallowed. "I...I can't bear to look at her just yet."

My chest tightens at the deep pain in his voice. I wait

for more, but he grows silent. His torment fills the empty void, breaking my heart. I can accept he isn't ready to delve into why, but remaining silent will not help bridge the gap he's built between himself and Apikalia.

"You asked what four times will do. For Apikalia—"

"Vivian."

"For *Apikalia*, since three times didn't work, she now believes that she has to poke you four times in a row to make sure you aren't dead. Because instead of reassuring her by waking up, you reinforced her fears. And for what?"

"What?" He swings around to face me fully, confusion and guilt hanging on him like an old sweater. "That makes no sense...but I guess it explains why she keeps doing it. How do I get her to stop?"

"If what I suspect is true, you'll need to find a professional to help her, and you'll have to play your part. You have to really want her to improve and not just to make your life easier."

He scrubs at his face. "Make my life easier? Nothing has been easy for me for years. She isn't even my kid." He drops back onto the couch as if the only thing holding him upright until now was his resistance to a small child.

I want to harden my heart to him for denying her so easily, but the anguish and longing in his voice tug at my sensitive organ. When will I learn to be objective? It is my best and worst quality at work.

"What do you mean by that?"

He sighs, his head hanging low. "While I was deployed, my wife slept with another man. The timing made it impossible for her to claim me as the father so she had to confess. What she did broke me. She was the love of my life since junior high. Then she went and died on me before we could discuss the whys and hows or resolve anything. How was I supposed to heal without her?"

"What she did was awful, but that has nothing to do with Apikalia." I sit and take his hand without thinking. Yesterday's tingling resurges and the burned cinders begin to kindle anew now that he's shown me that he isn't a cold-hearted bastard with no regard for his daughter.

He squeezes my fingers. "It has everything to do with her. She wears my wife's face. Every time I see her, I have to relive the unforgivable."

"I'm going to say this as gently as I possibly can." I wait for him to raise his head and look me in the eye. "Get your head out of your ass. Apikalia is a niñita and she needs her father. If there's one thing your mother taught me, it's that la familia does not stop at the blood flowing in our veins. That girl has no one else, and I want to believe the man Makana praised still exists. Don't you?"

"Of course I do." Hurt peppers his voice and he surges from the couch, leaving me to watch him pace in agitation. "I don't know why I'm telling you this. Maybe I'm tired. Fighting enemies on a battlefield is less taxing than fighting myself every damn day."

Keoni walks to the kitchen and returns with an open beer bottle. It is already half empty. The desire to comfort him rises inside me again, stronger than the last. I don't understand why he generates this reaction in me, almost as if we've met before and I know this version of him isn't the real him. This time I control the impulse to go to him.

From his tightly wound frame, Keoni's been holding back these feelings for a long time, and I won't stop him from lancing the wound that has been festering for years. It's a miracle he hasn't become an abusive bastard. Then again, neglect is its own form of abuse; a hard lesson I learned from my father that I don't want Apikalia taking to heart.

"Ever since I held her in my arms as a newborn, I've felt like I've had to rip my heart out just so I can survive each day. Isolating myself from my family, taking every PCS post when deploying didn't cut it, any and everything to distance myself physically because I knew that was the only way I could get through the day."

"Wasn't there anyone you could talk to?"

He scoffs while peering at me as if in search of a truth I don't possess. "I thought I'd found someone. That I was close to leaving the past where it belonged, but reality has proven time and again that I don't deserve to be freed from this burden."

Losing a confidant must have been horrible for him during his hopeless moments.

"Since I've overstepped the line about five miles back, I'll continue with this. Not to be callous because what you went through sucks like a sack of moldy dicks. But it sounds like you haven't moved on because you haven't forgiven yourself for your role in the breakdown of your marriage."

"My role?" He laughs a bitter and sorrow-filled chuff that grates against the emotions I try to reinforce with cold steel.

I am failing at being impartial.

"How am I supposed to know what I did to make her fuck some stranger? She isn't alive to tell me."

"Necesitas madurar," I say, marching over to him and poking him in the chest with the best tough love routine I can muster. "Be an adult. What you're talking about is confirmation. I bet you've always wondered if it was that one thing you did or didn't do all the time that blew up into a huge thing for her. Well, assume that was what got you two on the path that ended things and forgive yourself."

"It's not that fucking easy," he growls, his body expanding to encompass the entire room.

With the heat of his glare singeing me, I say, "I never said it would be. But you're a hard worker. If you put your mind to it, you'll figure things out."

His body deflates to its usual overwhelming size instead of the world-consuming one of moments ago. "How do I do that in time to help Vivian?"

"Multitask. Work on yourself and support her while she works on herself. No one can do this job for another person."

His dark gaze ensnares me with his vulnerability, and I can't look away even if I wanted to. "What makes you such an expert, anyway?"

"I'm not," I whisper, trying to understand what is happening to me. I clear my throat and avert my gaze because staring into Keoni's eyes too long is hazardous to… well, a lot of things. "Which is why I suggested you find a professional. However, I am a social worker and can iden-tify when a child's emotional, physical, and mental needs are not met."

"Social worker?"

"Yes, I work at Apikalia's school."

"You can't take her away from me."

Chapter Three

Dear John,

I'm so glad your current deployment allows you to receive mail regularly. I've come to depend on your letters as much as you rely on mine. Seeing your name on the envelope always jump starts my heart because it means you are safe for another day.

I spend way too much time thinking about you in between correspondences, and I probably shouldn't have written that, but it's how I feel and I'm not ashamed to say it. So why should I fear putting it down on paper?

When thoughts of you overcome me, I bake some of my favorite childhood desserts. My abuela and I used to bake them whenever my father "forgot" about really important milestones in my life. I would start the day off crying or having temper tantrums, but end the day with a cold glass of milk, a pastry, and lots of laughs. She really knew how to turn something sad into something happy.

I hope the batch of mantecaditos and polvorones I sent do the same for you. They're from my abuelita's famous recipe books (only famous in my family), and I *figured cookies would stay fresher longer than my other specialties.*

Right now I am imagining you sitting beside me while we drink a glass of milk and bite into my creations. I think this will be enough to sustain me until your next letter.

Sincerely,
Fayth Love

A healing plan

How could I forget that my Fayth was a social worker? That this Fayth would be, too. Most of what I know about the people who practice her profession isn't good. They take children away. And given my knowledge of Fayth's ability to turn off her emotions and break promises, I can't trust her not to do the same with Vivian.

Gaining a new understanding of what lies beneath Vivian's fear and needing to undo the damage I've done in her short life takes precedence over her paternity.

"What tontería are you spewing now?" Fayth demands. "Have you heard a word of anything I've said to you? Take her away from you... Do you know the kind of damage taking her out of the only home she's ever known would do to la niña? She's already going through things adults can't manage and you think I'm going to traumatize her on top of that? Idiota!"

I can't deny the relief sweeping through me because I face a daunting task. I earned the rank of lieutenant colonel while serving my country, handled the health and safety of

1,200 men under my charge, and I fucking know how to tackle problems, no matter how impossible they may seem.

Yet a six-year-old is kicking my ass, and deep down I know I'm not equipped to handle it myself.

I stare at Fayth while memories of my most trying days play through my mind. Days where one letter from her made everything bearable. I may not have shared every detail of my life with Pen Pal Fayth, but I exposed more of myself to her than anyone else since my wife's death. Her ability to get me to open up hasn't worn off, only gotten stronger in person.

How else am I to explain why I opened up so quickly when I haven't shared my burdens with anyone for the last two years? I won't allow our history—a time that seems to have more significance to me than Fayth—to stop me from doing what's right by Vivian.

A part of me wants to yell at Fayth for taking my lifeline away or demand that she look at me and recognize me from my letters. But what good will it be to tell her the John from the marines she wrote to religiously is also the Keoni who is standing before her?

Not a god damn thing.

And right now, she isn't my priority.

"Will you help me with Vivian?"

She rolls her eyes and shakes her head at me. "Of course. First thing's first. Stop calling her Vivian. Makana gave her the name Apikalia for a reason. Use it."

"If you knew what her name means, you would understand why calling her Apikalia is difficult for me." I finish the beer in my glass and sit with my head resting against the couch's back.

"Should I fill the silence with nonsense until you enlighten me? I'm an expert babbler."

A smile tugs at the corner of my lips. "Apikalia is Hawaiian for father's joy. After I left Apikalia with my mother, she chose the name in hopes it will come true."

"Wise woman," she says as she plops next to me and leans her head against the couch.

Fayth has no idea. Makana Kekoa was wise and a wise ass.

"I think everyone who gets to know Apikalia learns what it's like to hold joy in their hands. You're lucky, because raising her means that one day you'll experience the same wonder in your heart and arms."

I twist around to watch as a wistful smile breaks out on Fayth's face. Just like that, the curve of her cheek and tilt of her lips transports me to the days I would frantically search my mail for her letters.

I rub at the ache in my chest, wondering... "Why did you stop writing me?"

The words that should have stayed inside my head ring in the silence between us.

Fayth turns to me, confusion writ on her brow. "What did you say?"

"You wrote to me for three years then all of a sudden, nothing. I practically lived off your letters. They pulled me out of a darkness I never thought I could survive. Then two years ago, you stopped. No warning. Nothing."

"However you found out about me, you need to stop." She cautiously pulls away as if I've turned into a rabid animal she can no longer trust to be in the same room with. "This isn't funny. First, you know how I spell my name without me telling you, now you're saying I wrote to you? I never wrote to a Keoni."

"No, you wrote to John Keoni Kekoa. Me."

With my revelation, she stops backing away. "John? No, my John didn't have a middle name."

My heart thuds at her possessiveness. *How dare she claim me after she discarded me?*

"I can absolutely guarantee he does. The question I want answered is how many Kekoas do you know?" I pause to suppress the anger I've carried for this woman since I realized no more letters were coming my way. "You never asked my mother if there was a connection?"

"Hey! I grew up in the Bronx. If I assumed every Lopez or Johnson was related, I wouldn't have made it past high school. I figured the same rules apply in Hawaii for Hawaiian names."

"You'll learn that's not exactly how it works here. Our community is small and locals like to know how we're connected. We don't ask out of a presumption that all Black people or all Latinx people know each other."

"I guess that makes sense. So, you're really John?" she asks with an odd note in her voice that I want to believe is hopefulness.

I slowly nod while downplaying the riot taking place in my gut between fury and yearning.

A frown wrinkles her brow. "But you never talked about a wife..."

I reach out and take her hands in mine, pulling her inexorably closer to me until she stands between my knees. "I never gave you her name, but I absolutely told you about her."

"The person who broke your trust?" Her eyes widen as she puts things together that I revealed in our correspondences. "The reason you couldn't come home."

"Yeah, all that."

"I thought I'd never..." Fayth fans her face, looking

toward the ceiling but she can't hide the sheen that appears in her eyes.

Although I desperately want her to finish her sentence, her shock is genuine. Her reaction wrangles the anger I've carried for years into a mute doll. All I'm left with is pining for a future I used to envision.

"Would you have told me more had we continued being pen pals?" Her voice catches in the middle of her sentence and she avoids meeting my gaze.

"Fayth, you had me believing I was ready to try again. I would have told you every embarrassing story that ever happened to me."

"But you stopped getting my letters." She frees herself of my hold and swipes at her lashes, leaving me bereft, but not for long.

She takes a bracing breath before kneeling on the cushion beside me and placing her hand on my arm. I cover her fingers with mine, drawing strength and comfort from her presence.

"It wasn't intentional," she explains while sympathy and regret warm her brown eyes and softens her mouth. "During the move, I lost your last address. At first, I didn't panic because I kept everything you sent me in a special cedar box I bought just for your letters. I trusted the movers to pack them, but I've gone through every box and have yet to find any of the letters."

"Wait here," I say and go into my room to retrieve a three-ring binder and hand it to her.

She opens it, paging through the laminated pages. "You really laminated them. And at the last stages, too. You can barely make out the words on this paper."

"I know every letter by heart," I profess, unafraid to

show her the feelings that have been brewing inside me for the past five years.

I take the binder back and prove it by flipping to a random page. "This is the letter you sent congratulating me on my promotion to lieutenant colonel."

The original blue ink is so faded that the paper looks like an impressionist rendition of waves. While staring her in the eyes, I recite the contents of the letter. No skipping or stumbling over words for me, but my voice thickens with emotion.

Fayth presses her open palm against her chest and takes another steadying breath. "You made that sound way better than what I remembered writing."

"Your words resonated with me then and still do today."

"Damn..." She blinks her eyes repeatedly. "I was not expecting this, but you deserve to know that I didn't just accept that I'd hired shitty movers. When I realized what happened, I tried to find where you were stationed and learned some things in the process. Like this fun fact, the military is really protective of their soldiers' privacy. I wasn't family and I don't have a huge circle of military friends. You're the only marine I know, and no one was sharing. By the way, do you have any idea how many bases there are? I wrote letters to as many as I could in search of my John. I guess I won't be hearing back any time soon."

"I suppose not."

"Wow! I can't believe you're here. In the same room with me." Fayth touches my face, her fingers a light brush against my eyelashes and nose. As wonder fills her eyes, her caress lingers on my lips.

"I'm beginning to think you got something way better than an address to mail letters." I sidle closer to her on the couch, no longer able to fight the growing need inside myself or my misplaced belief that I needed to hide what being in the same room with her means to me. Or my hopes reflected in her brown-eyed stare.

"Yeah?" she breathes.

"Definitely. And after today's heart-to-heart, I'm convinced we should pick up where we left off."

"Where...we left...off?" Fayth sits on her heels and lowers her hand from my arm. "Where was that exactly?"

I ignore the sense of loss from the connection she severed. Residual warmth reminds me of her touch and tempts me to pursue what I've been missing. "With me asking you on a date and you saying yes."

Chapter Four

Dear Fayth,

   On days like today, I wish I were closer to you or that I could hear your voice. How I wish I could hear your voice. We exchanged numbers ages ago, yet not once have we been able to connect and it's driving me crazy. Between towers malfunctioning, calls not connecting, or me being out of pocket, I'm beginning to think fate is fucking toying with us.

   I tried again today not realizing you would probably still be asleep because of the time difference. Am I a horrible person if I admit to wishing I'd woken you up because I want to hear what you would sound like in the morning?

   Let me stop because bitching about

stuff that's out of our control is a waste.

I wanted to thank you for the treats you sent me. The boys are on the lookout for your boxes now. It's my fault, really. I couldn't control my reaction when I bit into those guava cookies. I admit it. I moaned. And not once but every god damn time I took a bite. The jealousy is real and out of hand. I've had to threaten a few guys to keep their grubby hands off my cookies. Those greedy bastards can find their own woman to bake them treats. I'm keeping you and your bomb-ass baked goods to myself.

I won't lie. Some of my enjoyment comes from imagining your pleasure while baking. If picturing me fighting off my comrades also brings a smile to your face when an oven isn't nearby, all the better. Keep me in mind if your father continues his ~~fuckery~~ foolish behavior.

In the meantime, my body is aching after a grueling training, and although I could write you a book, I have to hustle if I'm going to eat or I'll have to wait until tomorrow morning.

Yours,

John Kekoa

A night to fall in love

The doorbell's ring pulls me from the current debate I'm having with myself in front of my closet. As I go to find out who is at the door, I can't help but wonder what Keoni has planned for us tonight.

I'm still unsure how or why I agreed.

Mentirosa!

Fine! The why is because he isn't the asshole I thought he was at first. After his revelations last night, I can only see him as my John from our many correspondences, the man I dreamed would cuddle me whenever my father sent me spiraling. With the knowledge of our shared past, the guilt I felt because of my attraction disappeared.

Still unsure if that is a good thing for me either.

Mentirosa! There's nothing bad about all your fantasies of him coming true.

Because knowledge of how his wife had hurt him opened my sympathy faucet and I want to wrap him in my arms until he is as strong inside as he is outside.

Girl, please. You want to climb him like Makapu'u Point.

I have little time to dwell on the shameful thought because on the other side of my door stands Apikalia.

"Hi, Auntie."

"Is something wrong?" I ask while searching the area behind her for her father.

"No, Daddy said I had to stay here until he was ready for the surprise."

I kneel on the floor to look into her eyes. "Did he tell you what the surprise is?"

There's no shame in grilling Apikalia for information. She and I are sisters for life now that she's told me Snugglepuss is really her cat and he only stays at my house to keep me company when she's busy.

She shakes her head and goes in search of my cat.

"He's in my room," I call out. "We were picking out my outfit for tonight. Want to help?"

"Yes!" She bounces in place, her enthusiasm rubbing off on me.

While I choose and discard outfits, I say, "Do you mind if we talk about what happened yesterday?"

"Yesterday?" she asks distractedly while playing with Snugglepuss and his cat toy.

"When you woke your father."

"Oh." Her body deflates and she bows her head, pausing her play to whisper the next like a shameful confession. "I did it again. I think I scared Daddy."

I leave the impossible job of choosing something to wear for my date and go over to comfort her on my bed. With my arm around her shoulders, I say, "Tell me what happened."

"I woke up in the night to use the bathroom but it was so quiet. I thought..."

"What did you think, amorcita?"

"That I needed to check on Daddy." She twists out of

my hold to face me and a wild look enters her eyes. "I had to wake him to make sure. If I did for Grandma she would be here now. But she never woke up."

Oh, Dios!

My heart tears as she raises a tear-filled gaze.

"Daddy says it's not the same and that I don't have to poke him because he's not going to leave, but he's wrong. I have to do it four times."

I cup her cheek, searching for the right words to ask what I want to know in a way she will understand. "Did someone tell you that you have to do this?"

She bows her head and shrugs. In a soft voice similar to when she made her earlier confession, she says, "I have a monster. Whenever Daddy's sleeping, the monster tells me he's not going to wake up."

"I see..."

The trauma from losing her grandmother triggered her anxiety. I'm not trained to help her, but there are a few things I can do until Keoni finds the right treatment plan for Apikalia.

"Do me a favor, okay?" Once she raises her head and nods, I clasp our hands together.

Apikalia clings to my hold like I'm her lifeline.

I cannot fail her. "When the monster says someone isn't going to wake up, I want you to say it too. And you have to say it out loud ten times. Slow or fast, but make sure you say the same words ten times."

"I...can't. What if it comes true?"

"What if it doesn't? Try it once first. I bet you can because you're brave and you need your sleep."

Although she doesn't verbalize it, her skepticism is a physical wall separating us.

"How about I bet a flancocho that you can do it," I say,

bribing her with my favorite dessert.

"What happens if I lose the bet?"

"You have to draw your monster. Deal?" I hold out my hand for a shake and she tentatively lays her small appendage in mine.

"Deal."

I clap my hands, which startles Snugglepuss into a high leap off the bed, making Apikalia giggle as if all her worries have disappeared. "I still have to figure out what I'm wearing for this date with your father."

She gets on her knees to lure Snugglepuss from under the bed. "Daddy's wearing shorts and an aloha shirt. Does that help?"

"It does." I choose a casual maxi dress that caresses my body without downright molesting my abundant curves. "Did he tell you where we're going?"

I've lost her to Snugglepuss, who is currently toying with the ribbon on her skirt. A quick shower and wardrobe change later, I go in search of the little girl who is no longer in my bedroom.

Noises from the backyard lure me outside and my body stalls at the transformation that's taken place in the span of minutes.

"When did you get here?" It's impossible to hide my amazement as my eyes take in everything Keoni put together.

A projector and screen are set up for a movie under the ʻulu tree. "For when it gets dark," Keoni says, following my gaze.

In front of my lanai is a fire pit. Surrounding it are blankets, my patio couch, a bed of cushions, and takeout containers. The romantic gesture reminds me of the thoughtful glimpses from his letters. His ploy is working on me, propelling me past where we'd left off in our correspondences and making me anticipate what is to come.

"I didn't have time to cook, which is probably a good thing. There aren't many stomachs strong enough to hold down the disasters I create in the kitchen." Keoni approaches me with his hands out.

Instinctively, I stretch mine to his and a little sigh escapes me when his fingers enclose mine. "Apikalia let me in while you were in the shower. You look amazing."

His eyes devour me with banked heat that sparks embers inside me. The evening is cool, yet my body warms insanely fast. His appreciation makes the extra time I spent on my hair worthwhile. My curls are in a sleek faux mohawk with a bang falling just above my eyes.

"So date night is at my place?" I try to distract myself with conversation because staring up at Keoni's strong features or how the pressed aloha shirt flirts with his muscular build will get me in trouble.

I doubt a six-year-old is an effective chaperone.

"I hope you don't mind. After what we talked about yesterday, I'm not comfortable leaving Viv—Apikalia with anyone right now. And I thought this would be a good way to get to know my daughter while we reacquaint ourselves."

"I don't mind. I actually prefer nights in to out."

This man is effortlessly wiping out the horrible first impression I had of him. Does it count as a first impression if we've met through a pen pal program? I'm not sure, but my heart is singing a happy tune from knowing he's the same great guy I'd fallen for long distance.

"Yeah, I also remembered you mentioning that in one of your letters." Keoni pulls me toward the blankets.

I smile at him, a bout of shyness overcoming me all of a sudden. "So...um, what's for dinner?"

"I hope you like local-style Korean."

Now that I'm closer to the setup, I'm amazed at the number of containers.

My wide-eyed stare prompts Keoni to sheepishly admit, "I may have ordered too much."

He's not kidding. There's seaweed soup, a slew of banchan options ranging from kimchi to spicy daikon, meat jun, kalbi, mandoo, japchae, and tteokbokki.

"A little bit of everything won't hurt." I smile and sit on the ground with my back supported by the couch.

With Keoni beside me, a sense of rightness sweeps over me. I'm meant to be here beside this man, being pampered by him, helping him navigate his daughter's anxiety.

"Here, let me." He grabs a plate and begins dishing out food. "Viv—Apikalia, come and eat. It will take some time before calling her Apikalia becomes a habit, but you were right, it's for the best."

Apikalia comes running with Snugglepuss chasing at her heels. Keoni hands her a plate and she begins to eat. She appears so carefree that I almost forget that she has to be a little warrior sometimes.

Keoni hands me a plate and we dig in. The food is enjoyable but the silence between Keoni and his daughter doesn't sit right with me. I nudge him and motion towards Apikalia with upraised eyebrows.

He scrunches his face in confusion so I mouth to him, "Talk to your daughter."

"We don't talk during chow," he mouths back, making me realize that mealtimes must have been pretty somber affairs since his return.

"This isn't chow. This is your opportunity to get to know your daughter," I respond in kind.

"What do I say?"

"Idiota," I affectionately whisper with a shake of my head. "Apikalia, is there anything you want to do with your dad on King Kamehameha day?"

"Grandma always took me to the parade," she replies.

"Mom used to take me when I was a kid, too."

Apikalia's eyes widen in wonder, which starts a spirited conversation between father and daughter. I sit back and admire Keoni as he lowers his barriers to get to know his daughter. Apikalia's enthusiasm is equally moving as she discovers similarities with her father.

After dinner, the sky darkens, prompting Keoni to start the projector. He sidles beside me and beckons Apikalia to sit on his lap. As the movie starts, Snugglepuss curls in my lap.

I sneak a peek at everyone, overcome by a sense of belonging unlike any I've ever felt before. To think I hesitated when Keoni first suggested this date. I'm glad I accepted.

By the time the movie ends, Apikalia is passed out.

"She can spend the night in the guest room," I offer. "If you don't want to leave...just...yet."

A wave of embarrassment drenches me from head to toe, heating my entire body. I duck my head and cover my eyes.

Keoni's chuckle tells me he finds my current predicament amusing. "Show me the way," he whispers, then lifts Apikalia into his arms. He is so large that his daughter looks like a doll in his hands.

I lead him to the guest room, feeling his presence across

my skin although he walks a respectful distance behind me. Instead of waiting for him to tuck Apikalia in, I escape to the backyard. I need the cool night breeze to clear my thoughts of all the possibilities now parading themselves through my mind.

Will Keoni want to move past talking? Kissing? A moan escapes me when I picture his lips on mine and his big arms around me. How will he taste? Will he be forceful or tender or a little of both?

My body reacts to the mini fantasy playing out in my head and I pace, hoping to relieve my pent-up energy.

Walking won't do shit for the kind of energy you've got stored up.

"Thanks—"

"Ahh!" I clutch my chest. My heart races under my ribs. "Don't creep up on me."

"Sorry, I didn't mean to startle you." Keoni takes my hand and draws me closer until he encircles my hips with his arms. "Forgive me?" An impish smile breaks across his face, mesmerizing me.

"I used to wonder what it would be like if we ever met in person. I'm glad we have the opportunity." My confession rips out of me but the embarrassment I expect doesn't appear.

"Me, too," he whispers.

We stare into each other's eyes and the distance between us slowly disappears. Anticipation builds in my belly and I become a body of unfulfilled wanting.

"You know what else I wondered about?"

I shake my head because words are beyond my abilities.

"What our first kiss would be like. After so many years, I'm tired of wondering. Aren't you?"

This time I nod because I have been half in love with

the paper version of John for so long. Now that the real John...Keoni stands before me, I'm not back to where I was as Pen Pal Fayth. I'm a country and a corner store past that point. So far gone that I'm willing to leap into any and everything Keoni suggests.

Chapter Five

Dear John,

I hope this letter finds you well. Unfortunately, I can't say today has been one of my best, but at least I get to write to you.

A student came into my office and I recognized the look in his eyes. Without going into detail about his experience, he reminded me of the dark days when I lived with my father. He's the main reason I got into my line of work.

I don't think I was an effective advocate today. I hate seeing my students living through the same situations I did. It doesn't help that my day started in the dumpster with my father breaking yet another promise he made me. Disappointment is my constant companion when it comes to him, so why do I still hurt when he resorts to form? I wish I could quit him.

More and more, corresponding with you is the best remedy to restore my equilibrium and peace of mind. Did you get the last batch of cookies I made? I admit that I end up smiling as I wait for them in the oven because I picture you in a knock-down, drag-out brawl over them. I *made extra this time for you to share, but I doubt you will. You've made it clear that you want all my cookies for yourself.*

Please tell me you aren't one of those people who will eat cookies with soda or orange juice. I'd be hard pressed to send you any more goodies after that level of disrespect.

Who am I kidding? It would be well worth the price if my baking brought a smile to your face. Until then, keep safe.

Yours,
Fayth Love

Whatever it takes

Every night since our date two weeks ago, Apikalia and I have dinner with Fayth. I'm trying not to rush her, but our kisses make me burn for more. Hell, everything about the woman fires my blood. The way her body melts into mine. The smell of shea butter and mango on her skin. The wild curls that put mine to shame.

Every day I have to rely on my hard-earned discipline to keep my hands to myself when my desire to memorize every dip and mound of her body chips away at my self-control. If not, I risk Apikalia walking in on me ravishing Fayth every which way.

Apikalia, my daughter...

I even have Fayth to thank for the progress I'm making with my daughter, who has always been innocent of her mother's actions. With Fayth's help, I found a child psychiatrist who is guiding Apikalia through her anxiety. And Fayth has helped me combat the shame I've been living with for punishing Apikalia for her mother's sin against me.

It took more time than it should have to understand Fayth's attachment to my daughter. Her subtle prompts to help me interact with Apikalia are more for her. Fayth's chance to rewrite the loneliness she'd shared in her letters. Times where she reenacts conversations with her absentee father, but instead of the constant disappointments from the man who was too selfish to show up for his only child, she gets the love and attention she deserved.

The path I walked led to darkness until my take-no-prisoners neighbor held the mirror to my face. I hated what I saw, but every day since I've had smidgeons of proud moments that will one day give my daughter the confidence she needs.

Tonight, I've invited Fayth to my house for our date. The thought of leaving Apikalia with a babysitter does not sit well with me. I worry about her anxiety. She still checks on me at night. Sometimes I wake up to find her whispering the mantra Fayth and her psychiatrist taught her. Sometimes her therapy works and she goes back to bed.

Sometimes it doesn't.

When I wake to her poking me, I no longer try to interrupt her. Doing so only increases her stress and I won't risk her increasing the number of pokes for my comfort.

A knock at the door draws my attention from the table I'm setting. The food I ordered is warming in the oven.

"I'll get it," Apikalia yells. Her footsteps pound the wooden floors toward the door.

She greets Fayth while I quickly wash up.

"Hello, amorcita." Fayth's voice is full of tenderness that reaches me in the half bath.

Hiding my excitement doesn't cross my mind as I rush to meet the woman who has a chokehold on my happiness, has had me in her grasp since she voluntarily sent my unit an extra batch of cookies. Although only two weeks have passed since discovering her identity, my feelings for

Fayth have never died. Who can resist a woman who considers everyone's needs, including those of my comrades?

I come to a standstill at the very first sight of her.

Fayth wears an off-the-shoulder dress with cutouts at the sides revealing her deep warm-brown skin. The skirt of her dress has a slit exposing her thick thigh. I curl my fingers to stop myself from reaching out and grabbing her.

"Hi," she says with a knowing smile that jump starts me into action.

I don't stop until I'm almost on top of her. Fayth stands her ground but she can't hide the desire darkening her eyes.

"Did you wear that dress for you or me?" I whisper near her ear.

"That depends," she answers, her smile growing broader.

"On?"

"What happens after dinner." Fayth pats my chest and passes me. "Apikalia, what's for dinner?"

"Daddy bought butter mochi," she responds, taking Fayth's hand and guiding her toward the dining room.

"There's also real food," I call as I follow them.

Dinner is a test of endurance that I haven't faced in a long time, and Fayth is actively undermining my good intentions. She plays coy, as if touching the spot right above her clavicle isn't meant to draw my eye to her breasts. Or by twirling her hair I wouldn't focus on how kissable her lips are.

Time races by. Suddenly it's Apikalia's bedtime. Fayth assists me in bathing and putting my daughter to sleep, and all I want is for time to stop right now. To bask in this familial moment that I never dreamed would come true.

Outside Apikalia's door, I pull Fayth into my arms.

"Have I thanked you for everything you've done for me yet?"

"What? Tonight wasn't a thank you dinner?"

"You've got jokes."

"Well if you really want to thank me, you can stop teasing me." Fayth presses a forefinger against my mouth.

"Like this?" I ask before I suck her digit inside.

Her breath stutters and eyes dilate. "Keoni..."

Slowly, I draw her finger out of my mouth and spin her towards my bedroom. She leads and I follow, mesmerized by the sinful roll of her hips.

We've been building up to this moment for weeks and my tether snaps.

As soon as I get her into the bedroom, I press her against the closed door. "You have to promise not to wake Apikalia. Can you do that?"

Fayth licks her lips and nods.

I swoop in for my kiss. She rises to meet me halfway. This is what I've been missing all day. Although discovering Fayth is the same now as two years ago serves as a soothing balm, the knowledge doesn't dampen my ardor. Not after being deprived of her presence for the years before her final letter reached me. I have to act on all the repressed fantasies that kept me company from when I admitted to myself that she was more than a pen pal.

I bite Fayth's bottom lip until she opens her mouth to me. Any semblance of control deserts me. Without separating our lips and tongues, I lift Fayth by her thighs and she wraps her legs around my waist.

If forever were a place, it would be here and now where I can glut myself on everything Fayth has to offer. Her compassion, loyalty, and yes, her body.

I press into her groin, rubbing my hardened dick against

her pussy. The thin layer of her dress does little to dampen the sensation of being this close to my delightful obsession.

If my daughter chooses this moment to interrupt us, I'll go mad from unquenched desire, but Fayth's sweet mouth will make my descent worth every maddening second.

"You're wearing too many clothes," she pants while frantically pulling at my shirt, providing me with a few seconds of clarity.

I take her to the bed where I lay her down.

She stops me from pulling away completely by grabbing my hand. "You're going to want to see this."

My eyes drift down her body as she spreads her legs. Then she flips the split over her thigh until she exposes what she's been hiding all evening.

I swallow hard. "Should I be grateful you didn't tell me you weren't wearing panties?" I drop to my knees in front of her glistening flesh.

"A girl has to come prepared."

I glide my finger between her labia, inhaling her intoxicating scent. "There's preparation and then there's cruelty. How long have you been this wet?" I raise my hand and the light shines off the evidence of her desire.

"Who knows anymore? This is my new normal ever since you kissed me. Whenever thoughts of you run across my mind, I imagine all the ways you'll take me. Back when I only had your letters, you were my mysterious nocturnal visitor, too."

"Do you touch yourself?" I lightly run my thumb up and down her folds, delighting every time she takes a deep breath.

"No. I bear it because I don't want to come from a fantasy of you. I had enough of that when all I had was the paper version. When we come together, I need the real Keoni fucking the real Fayth."

Unable to resist the banquet in front of me, I lick her pussy. "I'm going to end your wait."

Fayth raises her hips but I withstand the urge to take another taste, though my body is raging at me for denying myself.

"Understand this. After tonight, there's no going back. We're a unit...family. You and I sleep together, wake up together, eat breakfast and dinner—"

"Together. Yeah, I get it. Now will you give me what I need or do I have to beg?"

My dick twitches at her suggestion, but that will have to play out another night. I can't tease her in the manner I want when I'm barely holding my shit together.

I release the weak restraint that has kept me in check until now and suck on Fayth's clit. Her thighs lock around my ears and I could happily go in this position. But not before Fayth.

I lick between her slick folds, swallowing every drop of her essence, not for a second taking it easy on her. Over and over I return, memorizing her taste and luxuriating in her arousal permeating the air.

She grabs a pillow and smashes it against her face to muffle her squeals of pleasure. I have found my new favorite hobby, because I can imagine spending hours, if not days, licking and sucking her while she drenches me in her pleasure.

With her free hand, she grasps the short curls on my head that have grown since my retirement, pulling at my scalp. The sharp sting zings through me, reverberating in my dick and causing me to groan into her folds. Fayth pumps her hips, her actions frantic and sporadic while she tests the sound-dampening powers of the pillow covering her face.

One day, I'll take her where we won't have to worry about interruptions. Where she can scream her pleasure with no one the wiser. Where my name will spill from her lips in a eulogy at the top of her voice. Until then, her shaking thighs tell me she is close and I double my efforts to push her over the precipice.

In seconds, she's falling. Her back bows off the bed and she releases my head to clutch the pillow with both hands. I take in the beauty of her orgasm while greedily licking her cum from her pussy and thighs until her shaking settles to intermittent trembling.

I don't care how messy my face is, I will waste none of her nectar while I clean her with my tongue.

When her legs fall slack and her chest rises and falls from exertion, I disrobe and retrieve a condom from my nightstand.

Fayth weakly pushes the pillow off her face. "So glad I waited."

I would laugh but her slumberous eyes and flushed cheeks steal my humor as something darker rises inside me. I stand between her legs and play with the slit of her skirt. "How attached to this dress are you?"

"I kind of have to be very partial to it. All my clothes are in my house and I'm not really the walk of shame in bedsheets type."

"Shame? I think not." I rip her dress from the split up her body until it comes away in my hands.

"Keoni!"

"Tomorrow when you walk to your house, it will be with pride while you wear my shirt." I lean over Fayth and kiss her nose, traveling past her lips. "Later, Apikalia and I will help you pack your clothes. There's plenty of space in the closet waiting for your things."

Her breathing turns erratic and her skin breaks out in goosebumps when I pause above her nipple.

"You're not wasting any time, huh?" she breathes.

"Haven't we waited long enough?" I engulf her bud and suck to the sounds of Fayth's pleasurable moaning.

"Dios! That feels good." She grabs my curls and presses my face deep into her chest.

I continue to kiss down her stomach; my mouth waters for another taste of her.

"Oh, not this time." Fayth pushes me on my back and straddles me, grinding her pussy along my shaft.

I instinctively grab her hips and clench my teeth against the intense pleasure of her wet slit sliding against me.

Fayth grabs my dick and positions me at her entrance. With her gaze impaling me, she sinks onto me. "Mmm." Her head falls back; her eyes close in ecstasy.

I clamp my fingers around her ass as I fight to control the overwhelming pleasure that comes along with stretching her until I'm deeply seated inside her. Fayth doesn't give me time to adjust, but I can't fault her because our coming together is long overdue. Her inner muscles pulse around my shaft in the most pleasurable way.

She places her hands on my shoulders, which is all the warning I get before she winds her hips and bounces on my dick. As much as I want to close my eyes and experience every sensation, watching Fayth take control of her pleasure fills me with more satisfaction than a quick orgasm can.

Her pussy squeezes my cock in its soft confines and her wetness slaps every time we come together, building heat between us. As she drives me out of my fucking mind, she lowers her mouth to mine. I open on instinct, allowing her to take whatever she needs, everything she needs.

Tonight I'm making her a promise with my body.

Fuck that.

I pull at her head despite her resistance to free our mouths. Once she leaves off mauling my mouth, I frame her face with my hands so she can see and hear my sincerity.

"Fayth, all my tomorrows are yours. Do you understand what I'm saying?" I search her eyes, hoping to see the same level of commitment.

She stops moving and my dick pulses inside her. Fayth takes my hand from her cheek and places it over her heart, rests her other hand over my heart, and gazes at me with a melting smile.

"You're entrusting your heart and faith to me. I promise to safeguard both because I can't imagine not having you in my life again. I'm in love with you, too, and you already have my heart and trust."

Fayth punctuates her declaration by swiveling her hips. With our hands over each other's hearts, she continues to pump her hips up and down my shaft. Our hearts beat in sync, and this more than anything pushes me closer and closer to coming.

Her moans come more frequently, and I can't help but grit my teeth as her motions become more and more frenetic.

With a cry, she comes, transfixing me with the power overcoming her. Her mouth freezes in a silent scream and her eyes flutter as wave after wave crashes through her. I fight my own need to close my eyes and let my orgasm overtake me. It's a close battle because her walls pulse around my dick, bringing me closer and closer to sweet madness.

My control snaps. "I fucking love you," I cry.

Without disconnecting our bodies, I twist until she lies on her back and I drive into her until my balls pull up. We kiss until my lips go numb, but it doesn't stop me from mindlessly sinking into her over and over.

I come, my soul emptying into the condom with my cum, and I wish the barrier didn't exist. My consolation is she's just promised me a future with her, and I intend to fill her with all of my love from now until I take my last breath.

Chapter Six

Dear Fayth,

You have no idea what your words do for me. They are the extra push I need whether I'm in training or out in combat. Keeping safe has become my secondary mission after I pledged to protect our country because I never want to make you sad.

I probably don't deserve your friendship but I don't care. Reading your letters and having imaginary conversations with you—yes, I do that —sustained me through some of my darkest moments, the ones I can't talk about with anyone.

Just yesterday I heard your voice, or what I imagined you sounded like, telling me not to hide from my emotions but to confront them, to embrace them, and to forgive myself for them. Since it's advice you've given to me that worked before, I tried it again. Hearing you in my head really hit me in the solar plexus this time and pushed me to work my shit out.

I would have written to you about it last night, but this emotional stuff takes a lot out of me; more than my regular PT. But when I woke up with my chest feeling lighter, writing to you was the first thought I had.

Who am I kidding? You're always my first thought of the day and the last before I close my eyes. Until our first phone call or face-to-face meeting, know I'll be thinking of you.

Yours now and always,
John Kekoa

All in

"Shhh." Keoni presses his finger against my lips. "Apikalia still bursts in on me in the bathroom. If you don't want her coming to investigate, keep your voice down."

He shuts his bedroom door and pulls me toward the bathroom. This is the first time since waking up that we're stealing more than a few seconds for ourselves. While Apikalia lies like a beached whale on the sofa watching TV, Keoni and I are going to freshen up.

Or that's what I thought the plan was.

The cool shower beckons me after the many trips between my place and his with my arms full of my closet's contents. Keoni even suggested moving some of the bigger furniture.

Keoni was not kidding around last night. He harnessed his days as a drill instructor to organize my mini move as if I would change my mind at any second.

I won't.

I can't.

I'm all in.

Why would I choose to go back to the emptiness of the last two years without him? I'm not a masochist.

But now I'm sweaty and in great need of cold water to wash away the stickiness from my skin. I'm not sure how clean I will get with the heated glare Keoni directs at me.

"Wait a second," I say before releasing his hand.

He arches his brow in silent question.

"I don't think your shower was built for us." I point between our bodies, his massively muscled build and my softer but wide and curvy body. I slowly walk backward toward the bathroom.

"We'll make it work," he says with a lascivious smile that makes my pussy tingle.

"Only if you catch me first." I shove him, knowing it won't do much good, then I sprint to the bathroom, intent on shutting the door on him.

His arm circles my waist and he twirls with me in his arm. "I win," he growls before slamming his mouth on mine.

There's no point in fighting him. He's won more than a race for shower rights. I will gladly be his prize. His tongue pushes into my mouth and I forget all about the acrobatic miracles we're about to perform just to share this shower.

Last night felt like a distant memory until this kiss. Our dancing tongues remind me that ecstasy awaits.

Keoni separates from me and I unconsciously follow his mouth for another taste. "When you're wet and naked you can have more." He pulls the shirt he gave me this morning over my head and tosses it into the hamper. Next, he drags the shorts he'd also loaned me down my legs. At my exposed pussy—because I didn't have time to put on a fresh pair—he pauses and inhales.

As if I wasn't wet enough, his obvious pleasure has liquid flowing between my folds.

"Why is there never enough time?" he mumbles, then takes off his clothes.

I enter the shower. He is not far behind. He wraps his arms around me and pulls me closer for another earth-shattering kiss. His dick presses into my stomach and all the desire to taste him runs rampant throughout my body, weakening my knees.

With one hand behind him, Keoni blindly fiddles with the shower controls until water rains down on our heads. I retreat a half step and lower myself to the tiled floor.

"It's your turn to be quiet," I say. While peering into his eyes, I take hold of his shaft.

Water splashes around his large body, protecting my vision of him as I engulf him in my mouth.

"Fuck that's—"

With my lips stretched around his dick, it's hard to smile at his outburst. I maintain eye contact and he tunnels his fingers through my curls. But he allows me to maintain control of how deep and how fast I take him.

I bob on his cock, losing myself in his intense stare and his salty essence. I suck at the veins protruding from the side and nip at his balls. Everything I do elicits him cutting off another curse or groaning my name or clutching my scalp tighter.

Each pull on my hair travels down to pulse in my pussy. "Mmm," I moan around Keoni's dick.

Tension builds within my body and I can't help the compulsion to rub my clit. With nothing stopping me, I give into the urge and massage myself. Each brush against the sensitive flesh has me purring, which causes a similar reaction in Keoni, who flings his head back.

He is beautiful in his pleasure, and I'm a fucking super siren because I'm in charge of giving him everything he wants. I become drunk on the feeling and continue to hollow out my cheeks as I suck on his dick.

Keoni taps my shoulders. "I'm going to come."

I ignore his warning and double my efforts until his abbreviated yell shatters the otherwise silent bathroom. His body convulses and I swallow every drop of cum, relishing in his salty flavor and imagining the next time I get to have him at my mercy. If I'm lucky it will be soon.

Keoni pulls away and leans against the wall, which causes water from the shower head to pelt me for the first time.

I smile up at him. "We should do this more often."

"Absolutely." He pulls me to a standing position and kisses me with abandon. "I should be mad at you for ruining my plans, but you can ruin them any day if this is what I have to look forward to."

I run my finger down his chest and tweak his nipple. "I aim to spoil you, Keoni. You're going to have to learn to handle that if you aren't ready yet."

His Adam's apple bobs as he swallows. "We better hurry before Apikalia bursts through the door."

Keoni washes me and I return the favor, lingering over every twitch of muscle as the washcloth glides over his dense frame. By the time we finish cleaning each other, I'm just as needy as when we entered.

That's fine. You appreciate the anticipation. Tonight when Apikalia goes to bed, shit is popping off.

I giggle at my inner slut who is already planning a thousand and one ways to blow Keoni's mind. I have to be prepared because he will do the same to me. I still haven't recovered from last night.

Keoni slides the shower door open, and sitting with an

avid stare in our direction is Snugglepuss. "How long do you think he's been there?"

"Who knows? How'd he get in? I thought you shut the door."

"Apparently, not well enough. Come on. As much as I enjoy seeing you in my shirt, you have your own clothes to change into."

I laugh at the pout on his face and go into the closet to get fresh clothes. When I return, Snugglepuss holds Keoni hostage in what I can only assume is a wellness check. The cat gently pats him down with a concerned look on his furry face.

I cover my mouth to stifle the laugh brewing inside.

"Go ahead. Laugh. I'm guessing he got concerned at the noises I was making."

"That aria you sang? I thought it was beautiful mysel—" A fit of giggles ruins my compliment and I double over.

Keoni leaves the cat to tackle me onto the bed, which flips the cat's concern to play mode. Snugglepuss pounces on Keoni's back.

"Oomph. Kiss me and I'll forgive you for laughing at my dilemma."

Without hesitation I do as he asks, curling my arms around his neck and my leg around his naked thigh to get as close to him as humanly possible. The kiss doesn't last long before he tears himself away from me.

"I need to dress."

I stare at his beautifully sculpted ass as he walks toward the closet.

"I can feel you objectifying me."

"Do you have a problem with it?"

"Only if you don't promise to keep doing it when we're both using walkers to get where we're going." He pauses at the door and peers back at me, his expression full of expectation.

"When it's time for those walkers, make sure you put a little extra strut in your hips when you walk away from me." I wink and he disappears into the closet with a hearty laugh.

Later that night, after we put Apikalia to bed, Keoni spoons me on the couch and we talk. My desire for him is a residual thrumming just waiting for the right moment to go into overdrive, but I'm in no rush. We're talking and I love getting to know more about him.

"I owe you an apology," I reveal, twisting around to look him in the eye as I seek his forgiveness.

He quirks his brow.

"Two weeks ago, when you showed up at my place, I nearly bit your head off, and it was an overreaction because of how I grew up. Without knowing you...or should I say, without knowing I knew you? Anyway, I painted you with the same bad brush as my dad because I envisioned similar heartache for Apikalia."

Keoni brushes his fingers across my cheek. "I figured that was the reason behind your reaction, but you still said a lot of things I needed to hear. I never meant to hurt my daughter, had become blind to what I was doing. I mean, even her name..."

"What? You mean finally calling her by her preferred name?"

"Not that alone." Keoni sighs and rests his head against the back of the couch. "Vivian is her mother's name. When Apikalia was born, I named her after her mother as a warning to myself not to get attached. Somewhere in my fucked up thinking was the rationale that saying Vivian's name would be the permanent reminder of her betrayal I needed."

Keoni lifts his head and spears me with his teary gaze. "Thanks to you, I'm not punishing an innocent girl for what her mother did, and I get to finally forgive my wife and myself for the many years of pain I've lived through. So, please, don't apologize. You put me on the road to healing, on the path to deserving you."

My heart twists with his heartfelt admission. Keoni doesn't have to try to be sexy, and I bet he doesn't realize what his emotional openness is doing to my libido. The low thrumming is now a raging, wanting beast with its eyes set on Keoni.

"Oh, wow. I don't mean to minimize any of what you just told me because it resonates deep within my heart. But seriously, could you say the sweet stuff while looking...you know...less sexy? I'm not supposed to want to take advantage of you after hearing that, but I totally want to take advantage of you right now. On this couch." I cover my face to hide my lack of embarrassment. "I'm shameless because I feel this way despite having a child in the next room."

Keoni drags my hands away to see the passion blazing in my eyes. "You had your turn in the shower. Tonight, I'm in charge of your pleasure."

He rolls over me and pulls me along into his bedroom. Before his lips touch mine, he asks, "Where's the cat?"

My frown of confusion spurs him to answer my unasked question.

"I don't need Snugglepuss pouncing on me in some feline attempt at protection. If he hears you moaning, he won't be curious, he'll attack."

"You don't...know...that," I respond while remembering a time when Snugglepuss tried to defend me against a former neighbor's dog. He'd come running at the sound of my distress and ran the much bigger animal off. "OK, you may have a point. We have to be wary about waking Apikalia and giving Snugglepuss the wrong impression."

We check the room to make sure we're alone before Keoni closes the door.

"Now, where are you supposed to be?" he asks.

"Face down, ass up?" I jokingly reply.

Keoni's eyes darken and a devilish smile spreads across his face. "I like where your mind's at."

I smile, knowing I will forever be by his side, no matter the obstacles we face.

Epilogue

Dear John,

I can't tell you how distressed I am. I've been sending letters to all the bases I can manage, trying to reach you because I've moved and lost your contact information. Life is toying with me because I have gotten no forwarded mail, but that would have made my life easy and we can't have that, now can we?

When I realized I wouldn't receive any more of your letters and I couldn't get in touch with you, I had the darkest moment in my existence. Darker than when I decided to permanently part from my father. I made the decision on the day of my grandmother's funeral and everything moved lightning fast afterward. By the time I had the words to express my turmoil, I was surrounded by a mountain of boxes with a new address and no way of letting you know how to get in touch with me.

You should have seen me digging through boxes and slowly realizing that my last connection to you was forever out of reach. It was then I understood I didn't just care about you. I've been in love with you, and now you'll *never know because fate and the post office are in league to keep me from declaring my feelings to you.*

If on the off chance one of these letters reaches you, please know that I'll be waiting for you.

Love,

Fayth Love

A family affair

"Keoni, there's a package here for you." Fayth walks out to the backyard where I'm grilling teri burgers. She holds a medium-sized, nondescript cardboard box.

I leave the grill, my curiosity aroused. "I'm not expecting anything." I check out the from address and recognize it as my last post before my discharge. "I'll open it later."

I'm on a mission and tonight Apikalia and I have big plans. Ever since Fayth gave up her rental next door and moved in with us two months ago, my daughter has accepted Fayth's role in our lives even better than I had hoped. Apikalia has blossomed under Fayth's unreserved love and protection. Much like I have.

As I watch my daughter chase Snugglepuss, the events from last week play out in my head. I'd picked her up from day camp to take her to the mall in Kapolei, an unlikely place to run into Fayth.

During the ride, I asked Apikalia, "What do you think about Fayth becoming an official part of our family?"

Although my eyes were on the road, I glanced in the

rearview mirror where Apikalia sat in her booster seat. She turned the biggest smile, showcasing her chipped front tooth. "Really? I prayed and prayed she would be my mommy."

"You did?"

"Uh-huh. Every night almost since I first met Snugglepuss."

"So did you want her to be your mommy or did you think she had to be your mom so you can get her cat?"

"Umm...both? I love Snugglepuss, but I really love Auntie Fayth."

Her reaction drew a chuckle from me. "I'm glad to hear you want her as a mommy. Want to help me make that happen?"

Apikalia's enthusiastic nod made me wonder how she didn't give herself a headache. That day, I swore her to secrecy, making her my Secret Squirrel with little hope of success. Surprisingly, Apikalia hasn't pulled a blue falcon and ruined our op. Her many questions of if today is the day notwithstanding, she's been a wonderful coconspirator.

"Apikalia," I call to get her attention.

Her gaze is curious but I can tell she wants to go back to chasing Snugglepuss.

"Can you get the super secret amazing thing we have?"

Like a light switch being flipped, her expression changes from one of mild curiosity to jumping enthusiasm.

"Today is the day?" she screams.

"Today is the day," I confirm, holding back the smile doing its damndest to break through.

Apikalia rushes into the house, her voice carrying no matter how far in she runs.

"Today is the day for what?" Fayth asks, a suspicious glint in her eyes.

"You'll discover soon enough." I seat her on an outdoor chair.

"Judging by Apikalia's reaction, it will be good. I guess I can wait to find out."

My daughter returns with her hands clasping her chest, hiding the big surprise we're about to unveil on the unsuspecting Fayth.

"Ready?" I ask Apikalia?

She nods enthusiastically and runs to my side. As one, we sink on bended knees and Apikalia holds out a ring box.

"Auntie Fayth, will you marry us and become my new mommy?" she asks.

I take the jewelry box from her small hands and open it for Fayth. "Yes, will you marry me and be my wife? I promise to be your bedrock like you've been for me. To stand with you and fight beside you no matter the obstacle. To—"

"Callate, ya! Idiota. Of course, my answer is yes." Fayth launches herself at us and envelops us in her arms. "We're already a family, but I like knowing I'll be a Kekoa just like you." She tickles Apikalia, who twists within her embrace.

My heart fills with more happiness than any man deserves, but I will greedily claim it. All the happiness in the world, my daughter, and Fayth. Who needs anything else?

The night passes with Apikalia cheering us with sparkling cider while Fayth and I drink champagne to celebrate. I can't take my eyes off the diamond on her finger, confident that she will honor the promise she is making to me and Apikalia.

Later, we tuck our sleepy daughter into bed. I herd Fayth towards our bedroom, but she slaps a hand across her forehead.

"I forgot the box outside. Let me bring it in so it doesn't get rained on tonight."

I sigh at the delay. "No, I'll get it. But don't think you can postpone what's about to happen behind that door once I return."

"Name the position."

Fuck!

"Any position will do, but I think we should start with plain old missionary. I want to look you in the eyes for every second of our connection. Watch your reaction when I profess my love while I'm deep inside you and your pussy clutches my dick. See when you can't hold out any longer and you come all over me."

Her breath stutters. "I-is that all?"

I kiss her nose and walk to the backyard with the biggest erection known to man. A few seconds of searching nets me the delivery from earlier. At the kitchen counter, my curiosity overrides my desire to join Fayth and I open the package with a butcher knife.

Inside are dozens upon dozens of letters. With shaking hands, I reach in the box to withdraw a hand-written envelope. The familiar cursive weakens my knees.

I tear into the first letter and read the contents greedily. I don't know how long I stand by the counter reading page after page of increasing desperation and love. So much love and concern that my heart is rendered in two and sewn back together much stronger than before.

"Keoni?"

I turn as Fayth approaches me, her concern transforming into alarm.

"What happened?" She rushes to me and brushes my cheek.

Only now do I realize that my face is wet with tears. I

kiss her hand then give her the letter, one of many she'd written me over the past two years.

"I'm sorry for making you wait so long for me. For not searching for you as hard as you searched for me. Had I known..."

"We found each other when we needed to. Let me take these, they aren't worth your tears."

I snatch the box out of her hands. "Don't you dare. You don't need to protect me from my feelings. Not when it comes to you or these letters. They are testaments to our love and I will treasure them forever, the way I'll treasure you and our life together."

Thank you so much for reading A Test of Fayth.

Please leave a review to let me know how you enjoyed Fayth and Keoni's story.

If you can smell peppermint and gingerbread cookies, that's because my next book is part of the Curves for Christmas collaboration. Join me in Bourbon, Texas for a Christmas to remember. Continue reading for an intro your new favorite Christmas novella, **Caught Red Handed**.

Caught Red Handed

October

"You don't need your apartment tonight, do you?" Honor asked over the phone, her unique mix of imploring and demanding coming through Yomaris' earpiece.

Yomaris was walking toward the parking garage's elevator bank when her sister made the request. She nearly stumbled over her stilettos, then righted herself, checking her surroundings for any witnesses to her clumsiness. Assured no one had seen her near miss with the concrete floor, she continued to the elevator's bright lights.

A list of reasons why Honor needed her apartment ran through her head in a matter of seconds. None of them boded well for Yomaris' blood pressure.

"Yoya?" Honor asked in the elapsed silence.

The elevator doors opened. Three men and one woman shared the small space. It took Yomaris two seconds to decide not to wait for the next car. She entered and situated herself in the middle, knowing she would need what awaited her upstairs even more once she hung up with Honor.

"Would it matter if I did?" Yomaris answered her sister in a hushed tone and glanced left and right, hoping the four people couldn't overhear her younger sister's end of the conversation.

"Not so much. So, you'll find another place to stay tonight?"

Yomaris sighed. "Do I get to know why I need to find somewhere else to sleep tonight?" She lurched as the elevator came to a stop, missing the woman in front of her by the grace of God.

Once the doors opened, Yomaris sped out, seeking some semblance of privacy in the popular hotel.

"Only if you promise not to lecture me about my life choices."

"Honor..."

"Yoya, it's just for tonight. I'll be out of there by the afternoon."

"But you know how much I hate wearing day-old clothes." Although she prevented herself from stomping her foot like an irate toddler, she failed to keep the whine out of her voice.

"Please..."

Anytime her siblings begged, Yomaris caved without a fight and often without explanations.

"Fine! On one condition. Tell me how much I'll need to pay to get you out of whatever situation you're trying to hide from."

"Give me a little credit."

Yomaris let out an audible groan.

"Okay, I needed two grand—"

"Honor..."

"You promised not to lecture."

"I did no such th—"

"Well, it was great catching up. I'll call when I'm leaving. Love ya, bye!"

"Honor! Hon—"

Her sister hung up, leaving Yomaris to blindly pace off her frustration and put on the bubbly personality she wore in public so she could check in to a room.

"Oomph!" Her face slammed into a hard surface.

The wall pushed her back with the same force as she had hit it. In the millisecond it took to recognize the wall she'd barreled into was a person, she also understood she was about to land on her ass. Hard.

A steel bar wrapped around her considerable waist.

Wait... can steel bars bend?

No, but the man who owned the immovable chest also owned the arm, preventing her from injuring her favorite attribute. In fact, said arm didn't stop when she was upright. Its owner continued to pull her inexorably closer to the wall of his chest, the broad surface only thinly covered by a straining button-down shirt. He stopped when they were chest to chest and her feet dangled slightly above the floor.

She raised her gaze, passing a pair of lips down-turned into a sinfully attractive frown and a nose with a bump hinting at a previous break, until she met the most stunning pair of emerald eyes she'd ever seen. The lushest set of natural, black lashes framed them, putting the ones she bought for herself to shame.

Why was she jealous of a stranger's lashes?

"You should pay attention to where you're going." The stranger's gruff tone made it clear he didn't appreciate being bumped into, but the gravely quality and the sexy Irish lilt played havoc on her senses, almost like a magical spell wrapped around them, inexorably entangling them together.

She shook her head of the whimsical thought and plastered a wide smile on her face. It was her signature, *"I can win the grumpiest of the grumpiest ogre over"* smile. The same one that helped her win over donors for her charity, MUEVE, better known as Manifieste Una Espléndida Vida Exitosa.

He stiffened, but she ignored the tightening hold on her back.

"You are totally right. I swear I need an alert system whenever I approach objects and people. The world would be a much safer place," she laughingly nodded, then began a cursory pat-down of his chest, shoulders, and arms. "I hope I didn't cause too much injury."

He loosened his grip until her feet landed softly on the tile floor, pink tinging his cheeks.

"It's a good thing you're so sturdy. I've taken down some pretty big structures—"

He grabbed her hands, the motion so abrupt it halted her speech and caused her to freeze while staring into his eyes again.

Her heart slowed to a sluggish thud before returning with a vicious beat she feared her handsome savior could hear. As hard as it was, she tore her gaze from him. That's when she realized why he'd seized control of her hands. She'd lowered them to his waist. Any lower and he would file assault charges.

Heat flooded her cheeks, which only made her nervous chatter worse. His measly eight words earlier didn't help matters either.

"Well then, it appears you are good to go. I'll be on my way, but if you're ever in the market for a near-fatal person-on-person collision, I'm the woman for the job. I'll be easy to spot, as I'll probably barrel into another poor, unsuspecting individual who only wants to go about his business," Yomaris said, backing away.

And, of course, she backed into a wall with an audible thud. She closed her eyes and groaned from the added embarrassment. When she peeked at him, he hadn't moved; his body as imposing as when he'd held her close and his expression as closed off as when he'd reprimanded her. But the twitching at the corner of his lips assured her he would not tear her a new asshole.

Good enough.

She quickly passed him with a friendly wave. "Good luck with the moving masses."

Five minutes later, she had a room booked which guaranteed her a bed instead of being relegated to the couch by Honor, who hogged the bed in her sleep. She sat at the hotel's bar, the stranger still preoccupying her thoughts.

Get your head right. He isn't why you're here.

She needed the reminder that she was here to celebrate and indulge, since she no longer had to drive home. Although she counted sweet-talking donors as an asset for MUEVE, she still struggled to get enough funding. But the universe decided to shine its warm, glittery goodness her way and bestow her with a valuation beyond her imaginings.

The haul she'd just stolen...er *relocated* to new owners was the best yet. The proceeds would help foster kids like her and her siblings adapt to life after they aged out of the system.

For a year, at least.

A good thing, too. As skilled as she was, thoughts of her last foster parents always overshadowed the jobs she took to help those around her. All the loss, pain, and suffering she survived as a child into early adulthood led her to where she was now. A successful CEO overseeing the mental, emotional, physical, and financial wellbeing of young adults leaving foster care.

Also, a woman about to commemorate her most recent "donation" with many adult libations. Definitely not a woman who wished to see what a strange man's frown flipped into a smile would do to his captivating green eyes.

There she went, thinking about him again because of some mysterious pull she couldn't explain.

This is the time to celebrate and reflect!

Yes, she should reflect. She took the last sip of her drink and ordered another with the raise of her finger. The bartender sidled up to her with a smile. She engaged him in a little flirtation while he poured her cocktail, but he was called away soon after.

Yomaris shrugged. It was expected on a busy night like tonight. She wished him lots of tips until it was time for her refill.

Then she turned her attention inward. Reflecting on completed jobs always helped hone her skills for the next heist and reassured her that she'd left nothing behind to tie her to the crime. With this one, she'd gotten the location and information that the owner was out of town from her usual underground contact.

When she entered the mansion, she recognized its potential. The house was a thief's dream.

The owner had to be a man. Dark, heavy furniture filled the large rooms with a modern and masculine feel. Steel accents and hidden gadgets were everywhere. His place was a challenge that had given her a high she was still riding.

When she made her way through, she thanked her contact, who had more than earned his ten percent cut. The home had a treasure trove of art and jewelry. She couldn't stop the impulse to take as much as she could pack in her vehicle.

As she relived her steps, going from room to room, she analyzed where she could improve, what tools would make things easier with the next job; the usual list of after-heist review she put herself through.

Nothing from her review left her feeling uneasy. With renewed peace of mind, she focused on her drink again, settling enough to celebrate. She had another four or five more drinks to go before she turned in, so she snagged the bartender's attention.

"You want something different this time, sweetheart?" he asked.

"I sure do. I'm ready for a serious drink," Yomaris smiled and winked at the man.

"I aim to please. What can I getcha?"

"I want a Suck, Bang, and Blow," she said in a sultry tone that made the bartender flush.

"Fucking hell! Don't even think about pouring that for her," the grumpy Irish voice from her earlier interlude said behind her.

She whirled her stool until she faced the owner of the voice, and...yep, he still wore that frown that shouldn't be as devastating to her senses as it was. She didn't even have the alcohol to blame for her body's reaction, since she'd only had two weak drinks to begin with. Only tequila could mimic the warmth running through her bloodstream, and he'd just nixed the cocktail with fermented agave as an ingredient.

No worries. Señor Malhumorado would not dampen her good mood.

She turned on her megawatt smile. "Well, look who's still upright and sturdy. I swear on this bar's good name that you can walk about without fear of me bruising your impressive physique." Yomaris winked.

A few seconds of awkward silence passed, during which he checked his watch. She opened her mouth to fill the quiet, but he grabbed her elbow.

"Come with me." Without waiting for her response, he pulled until she stumbled after him to an empty corner booth. He gently pushed on her shoulders until she sat, then he seated himself.

She had to scooch further into the corner to accommodate him and prevent herself from being pressed against his body. Not that she would mind. He had an impressive body, but satisfying her curiosity was more important at the moment.

"This was a good choice. I mean, if you manhandled me into this booth so you can talk to me without me accidentally damaging your person, I commend you. And with your arm span, you'd be able to hold me at a good distance at the slightest warning."

She would have continued on, even as the ticking in his jaw proved he was losing patience with her. But a waitress chose that moment to deliver glasses of water and bread.

Once the woman placed everything in front of Yomaris and the stranger, the waitress asked, "Can I take your order?" After one glance at Yomaris' companion, the waitress glued her eyes to the table's surface.

"Come back in five minutes," her taciturn amigo shot at the server.

The woman fled with a nod, as if she'd escaped a dangerous situation.

Curious.

The man shoved the basket of bread in front of her. She took that to mean *eat.* So, she selected a hot, yeasty roll and dug in. His gesture contradicted his surly behavior, exposing a level of caring that resonated with Yomaris on a deep level.

"You saw her reaction. That's typically most people's initial reaction to me." The man pinned her with his glare.

"O...okay? That's good to know?"

His nostrils flared.

"Do you want me to be afraid of you? I suppose I can try my hand at it, but I probably won't be much good. In high school, my drama class voted unanimously for me to work the box office. But if you want to risk being front row and center to my horrible performance, me da igual."

Instead of answering, the black-haired dream drank from his glass.

Yomaris leaned forward. "Are you a secret masochist?"

Water sprayed from his mouth and he began coughing. She started pounding on his back while wiping the table. Once he settled and glared at her, she sat back and continued her line of questioning.

"Is that why you don't mind putting your life at risk by sitting this close to me? Even coming to your rescue just now could have been more hazardous to your health."

"Stop. Talking." Redness slowly receded from his face, his recent bout of coughing leaving him none the worse for wear.

Finally, he turned his emerald gaze on her and began crowding her until her back hit the wall and she had nowhere to run.

"You should *fear* me, but you don't, and that intrigues me." His gaze traveled to her gold, black, and brown twists.

If the savage quirk to his lips and the darkening of his eyes were any indication, he was not having very innocent thoughts about her hair. Maybe he envisioned his hands wrapping around the strands and pulling her head back so he could take advantage of her gasp and plunder her mouth. Maybe while he was at it, flooding her mouth with his taste, marking her as his, he also happened to—

"I think after your little grope session, I'm not alone in my thoughts." His words shocked her from the little daydream that now had her squirming in her damp panties.

She followed his gaze to the nipples poking out of her shirt, advertising her body's need to be touched. She quickly covered her chest by folding her arms and cleared her throat.

"It would be kind of stupid to deny my reaction to you, but I must object to your allegation. I did not *grope* you. I assessed you for injuries. As a concerned citizen, I was only looking out for my fellow man."

"And this *fellow man* is going to have to insist that you repeat that performance. Nude. And for as many times as it takes to satisfy us."

Yomaris swallowed what liquid remained in her mouth. Because she was more than considering his proposal. Her body had screamed "hell, yeah" as soon as he finished his proposition. Her mind was running to catch up, but something had hamstrung her on the mad dash to *yesville*.

"I don't even know your name," she said.

For the first time, he smiled. Straight, even teeth that said if she were good, he'd be just as good to her, but he would much prefer her to be naughty. A new beat began drumming below her waist, and wetness seeped from her folds.

She was doomed.

"You want my name? Earn it."

At that moment, their waitress reappeared. Before she could utter a word, el Señor, which Yomaris decided she would call the mysterious stranger since he refused to give her a name, held her attention prisoner with his gaze and said, "She'll have the amberjack." To Yomaris, he said, "It will provide you with the energy you'll need for tonight without being too heavy on your stomach."

Yomaris, whose glance hadn't wavered from the enigmatic stranger, swallowed again. Had her earlier call with Honor infected her with her sister's penchant for making rash, illogical decisions? "I have a room upstairs," Yomaris offered, silently confirming that she and Honor had more in common than she'd previously thought.

And damn her if she wasn't looking forward to earning this man's name tonight.

What happened upstairs? You'll have to read it to find out.
https://www.amazon.com/dp/B0B4VB2TWC

Other Titles by Melverna McFarlane

Jessie & Giorgio: Inescapable (Oliveri Mafia Book One)

René & Nico: Inevitable (Oliveri Mafia Book Two)

Onika & Lorenzo: Indomitable (Oliveri Mafia Book Three)

Cantrelle & An Bao: The Making of a Ruthless Enforcer (newsletter exclusive)

About the Author

Melverna McFarlane loves love stories with Happily Ever Afters. After years of characters taunting her imagination with their potential, she decided it was time to write her own scorching hot romances. She moved to America from Jamaica at a young age, and has lived up and down the east coast most of her life. The bitterly cold winter of 2013 was the last straw, driving her back to island life—this time to Hawaii. When not writing, she is reading romance, YA, and Fantasy, country hopping, or vicariously obsessing over other people's cats, because she can't have one. She loves to hear from readers.

Join her on:

Patreon - https://www.patreon.com/MelvernaMcFarlane

Twitter - https://www.twitter.com/MelvernaM

Instagram -
https://www.instagram.com/melverna_mcfarlane/

Facebook -
https://www.facebook.com/melverna.mcfarlane

Website - www.MelvernaMcFarlane.com

Drop her a line, or tease her with pics and stories of your cat's antics. She might feature them in her next book.